MILLIONS OF YEARS AGO

the summers were so hot that they never seemed to end.

DINOTRUX ruled the earth!

The jungle was steamy, bugs flew everywhere,

and the Dinotrux were getting

grumpy and overheated.

They needed a vacation!

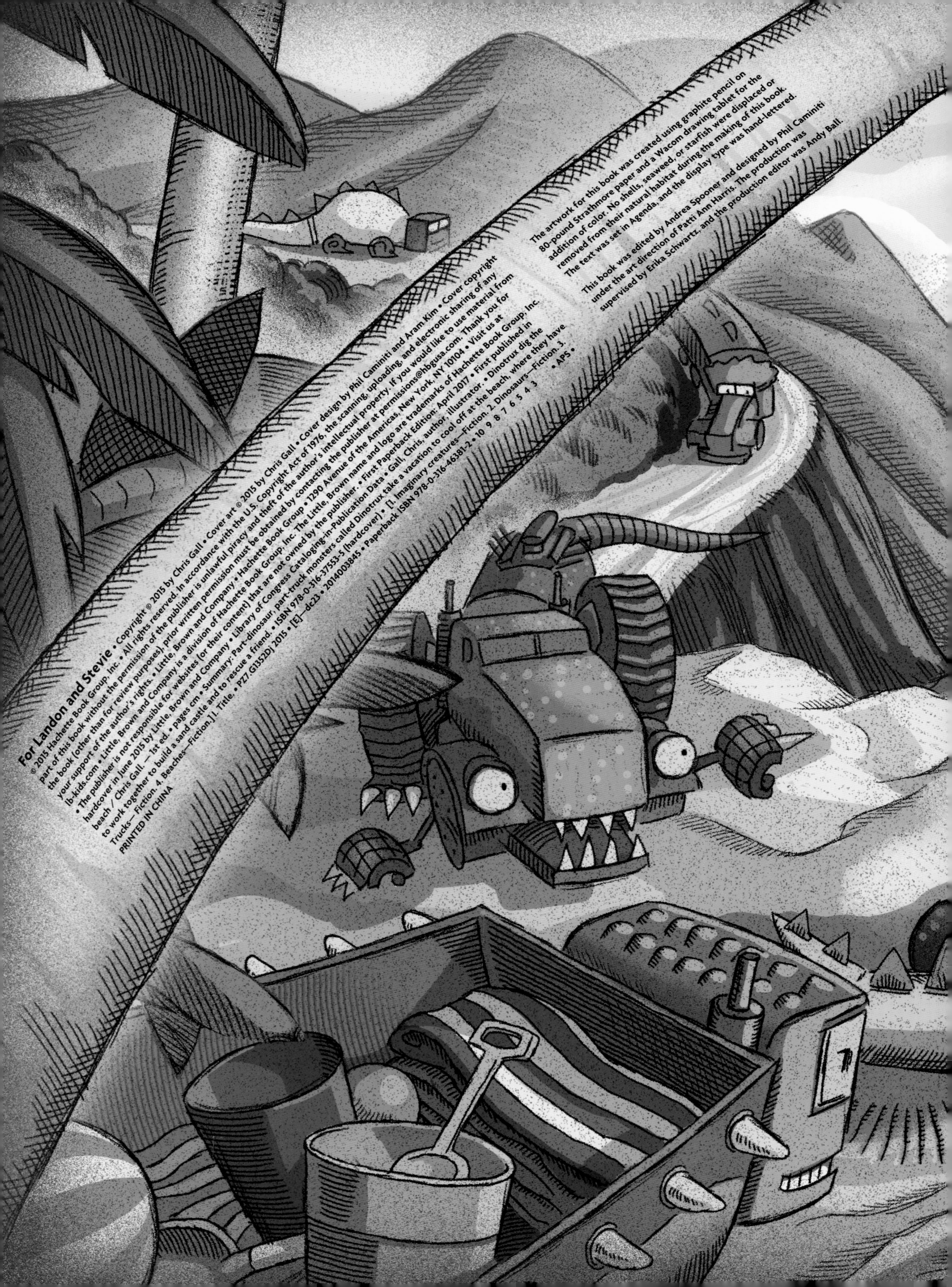

For Landon and Stevie

Little, Brown and Company • Hachette Book Group • 1290 Avenue of the Americas, New York, NY 10104 • Visit us at lb-kids.com • Little, Brown and Company is a division of Hachette Book Group, Inc. The Little, Brown name and logo are trademarks of Hachette Book Group, Inc. • The publisher is not responsible for websites (or their content) that are not owned by the publisher. • First Paperback Edition: April 2017 • First published in hardcover in June 2015 by Little, Brown and Company • Library of Congress Cataloging-in-Publication Data • Gall, Chris, author, illustrator. • Dinotrux dig the beach / Chris Gall. — 1st ed. • pages cm • Summary: Part-dinosaur, part-truck monsters called Dinotrux take a vacation to cool off at the beach, where they have to work together to build a sand castle and to rescue a friend. • ISBN 978-0-316-37553-5 (hardcover) • [1. Imaginary creatures—Fiction. 2. Dinosaurs—Fiction. 3. Trucks—Fiction. 4. Beaches—Fiction.] I. Title. • PZ7.G1352Dj 2015 • [E]—dc23 • 2014003845 • Paperback ISBN 978-0-316-46381-2 • 10 9 8 7 6 5 4 3 • APS •

PRINTED IN CHINA

The artwork for this book was created using graphite pencil on 80-pound Strathmore paper and a Wacom drawing tablet for the addition of color. No shells, seaweed, or starfish were displaced or removed from their natural habitat during the making of this book. The text was set in Agenda, and the display type was hand-lettered.

This book was edited by Andrea Spooner and designed by Phil Caminiti under the art direction of Patti Ann Harris. The production was supervised by Erika Schwartz, and the production editor was Andy Ball.

DINOTRUX DIG THE BEACH

Little, Brown and Company
New York Boston

One morning in late summer, **TYRANNOSAURUS TRUX** led the Dinotrux to a secret beach. The breezes were cool, and the waves crashed over the sand. The Dinotrux honked with excitement and plowed straight into the water!

CRANEOSAURUS poked his head under the waves and went fishing.

OUT OF THE WATER, DINOTRUX!
YOU'LL RUST!

The Dinotrux pulled themselves out of the surf.

DIGASAURUS immediately buried himself in the sand.

DUMPLODUCUS accidentally ran into a nest of crabs.

OUUUUCCCHHHHH!

The **DELIVERADONS** fell asleep in the sun.
Too bad they forgot their sunscreen!

GARBAGEADON went looking for food in a nearby tide pool. But the starfish had other plans.

CEMENTOSAURUS was so excited that he started to go. But the seagulls got him first!

DON'T LOOK DOWN!

Out in the water, **AMPHIBIDON** towed **SCOOPASAURUS** high into the air.

Then **ROLLODON** flattened some trees and made surfboards for everyone.

SURF'S UP, DINOTRUX!

That afternoon, TYRANNOSAURUS TRUX decided the Dinotrux should build the biggest sand castle ever. But the Dinotrux had never made a sand castle before.

When DIGASAURUS started to dig, the sand flew everywhere.

ROLLODON wanted to help. But he accidentally kept flattening their work.

And every time **DUMPLODUCUS** dumped his load of sand, the waves washed it away.

CEMENTOSAURUS thought it would be fun to lay the foundation.

TYRANNOSAURUS TRUX couldn't believe what he was seeing.

NO, NOT THERE!!

This was not the way to make a sand castle.

TYRANNOSAURUS TRUX roared
and assigned a job to everyone.
DOZERATOPS piled up the sand.
DUMPLODUCUS moved the rocks.
DIGASAURUS dug out the moat.
CRANEOSAURUS lifted the driftwood.

Finally, the Dinotrux stood back and admired their work.
It was the best sand castle they had ever seen
(even if it was the ONLY sand castle they had ever seen).

DUMPLODUCUS scratched the sand out of his moving parts. Something still seemed to be missing from their castle, but he didn't know what.

HMMMMMMMM...

Suddenly, the Dinotrux heard a tiny honk coming from way out in the water. They had been so busy that they hadn't noticed the tide coming in.

Little SCOOPASAURUS was surrounded by the sea and...

SHAAARKKKSS!

TYRANNOSAURUS TRUX to the rescue!
He roared and splashed into the water, scooped up the frightened little Dinotruk, and captured all those pesky sharks.

BOY, WAS HE TOUGH!

Then he found a great new home for them.

NOW the castle was perfect!

And as the sun set over the sea,
the Dinotrux hoped the summer would never end.